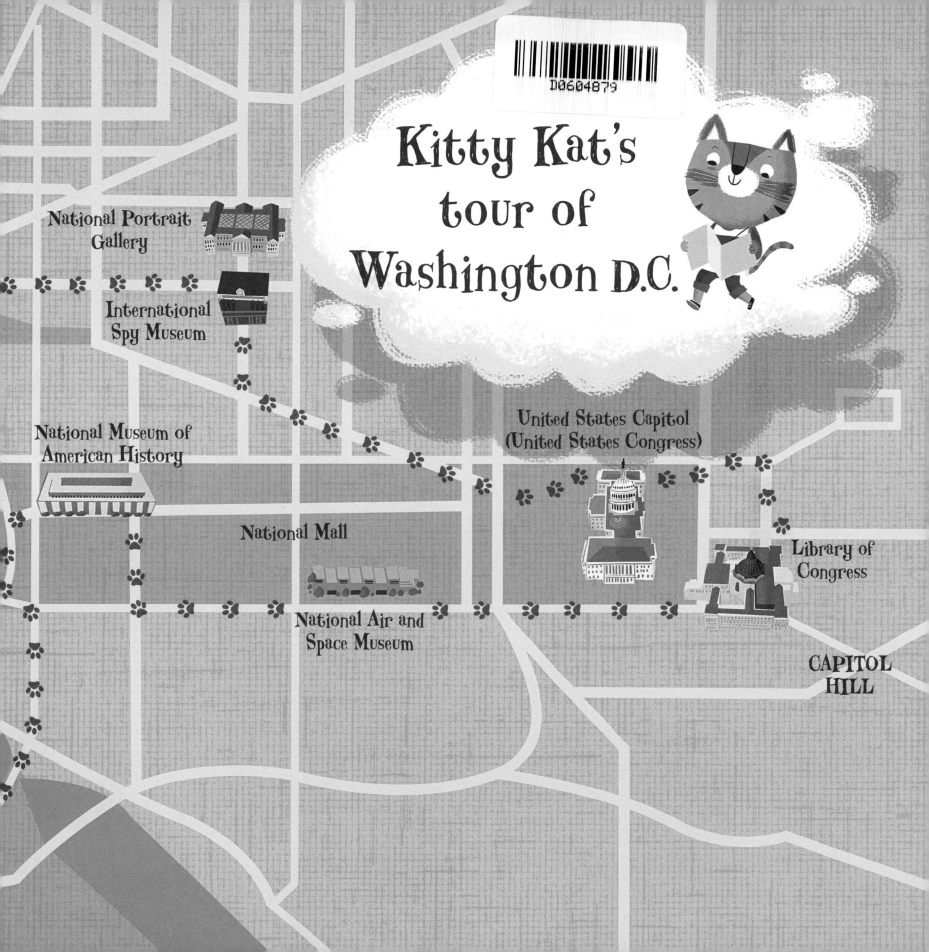

Kitty Kat, Kitty Kat, where have you been?

I've been to Washington D.C., and guess what I've seen...

Russell Punter

Illustrated by Dan Taylor

Kitty Kat, Kitty Kat,
where have you been?

I've been to Washington D.C.,
and guess what I've seen...

The city is full of great places to roam.
I began at the White House, the President's home.

Inside the West Wing, decisions are made.
The President works there, with help from top aides.

The grand Oval Office is named for its shape.
It's the President's office, where meetings take place.

In the National Portrait Gallery's halls,
great American heroes look down from the walls.

If you like secret agents and making up codes,
the International Spy Museum is <u>the</u> place to go.

The United States Congress is on Capitol Hill.
The people who work there make laws and pass bills.

The Library of Congress is well worth a look.
It's the world's biggest library, with millions of books.

In the National Mall you can stroll, jog or ride.
A long, cool Reflecting Pool runs down the west side.

There's American history, nature and art
in museums and galleries, right by the park...

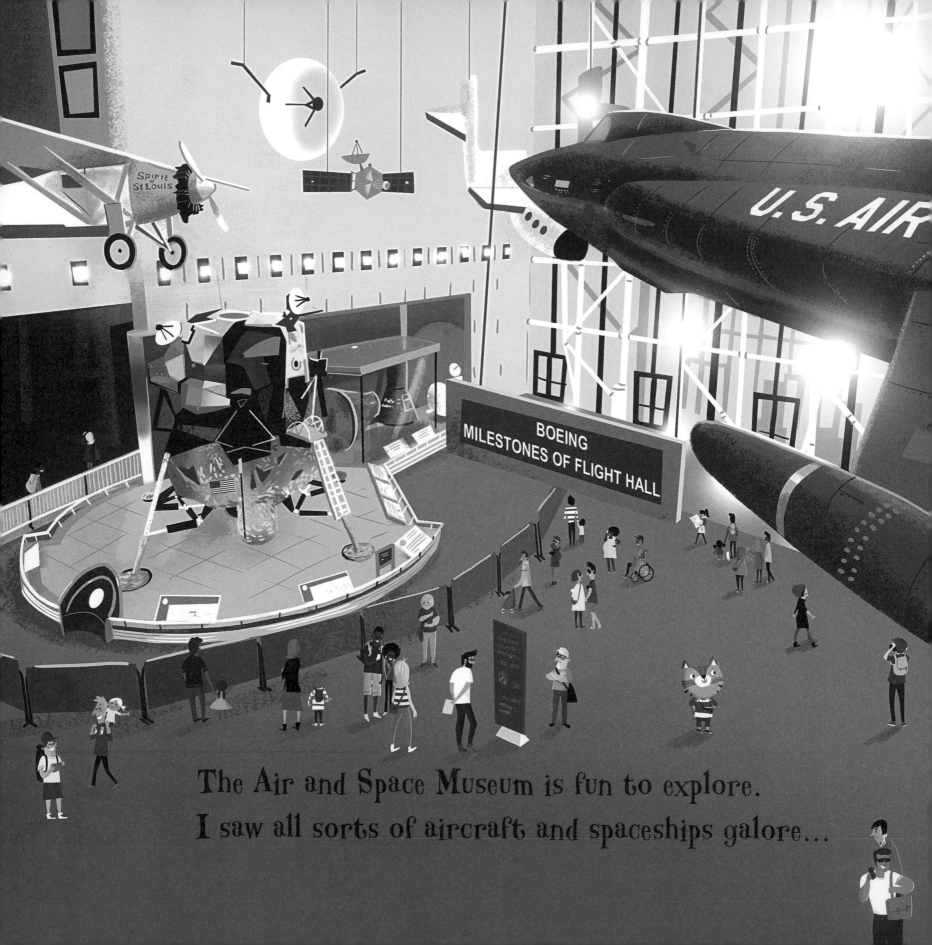

The Air and Space Museum is fun to explore.
I saw all sorts of aircraft and spaceships galore...

...there's the Museum of American History too,
where the Star-Spangled Banner is proudly on view.

The very first President's courage won fame.
The Washington Monument honors his name.

By the wide Tidal Basin, the cherry trees bloom.
If you visit in springtime, you'll smell their perfume.

Paddle boats on the basin will help you see more.
The Jefferson Memorial's right by the shore.

I cruised the Potomac, and stopped off to see
Theodore Roosevelt Island, where wild deer roam free.

At Arlington Cemetery, they were changing the guard.
It's a place to remember brave troops who fought hard.

At the National Cathedral, the stained-glass is cool.
On the special Space Window there's rock from the Moon!

Martin Luther King Junior thought folk should be free.
His Stone of Hope statue's a sight you must see.

IN THIS TEMPLE
AS IN THE HEARTS OF THE PEOPLE
FOR WHOM HE SAVED THE UNION
THE MEMORY OF ABRAHAM LINCOLN
IS ENSHRINED FOREVER

The Lincoln Memorial statue stands tall.
The President's speeches are carved on the wall.

There were thirty-six states, back in Abe Lincoln's day.
That's why thirty-six columns surround him today.

Well, Washington sounds like a great place to me.

You're sure to have fun if you visit D.C.

Edited by Jenny Tyler

First published in 2019 by Usborne Publishing Ltd., Usborne House, 83-85 Saffron Hill, London EC1N 8RT, England. www.usborne.com Copyright © 2019 Usborne Publishing Ltd.

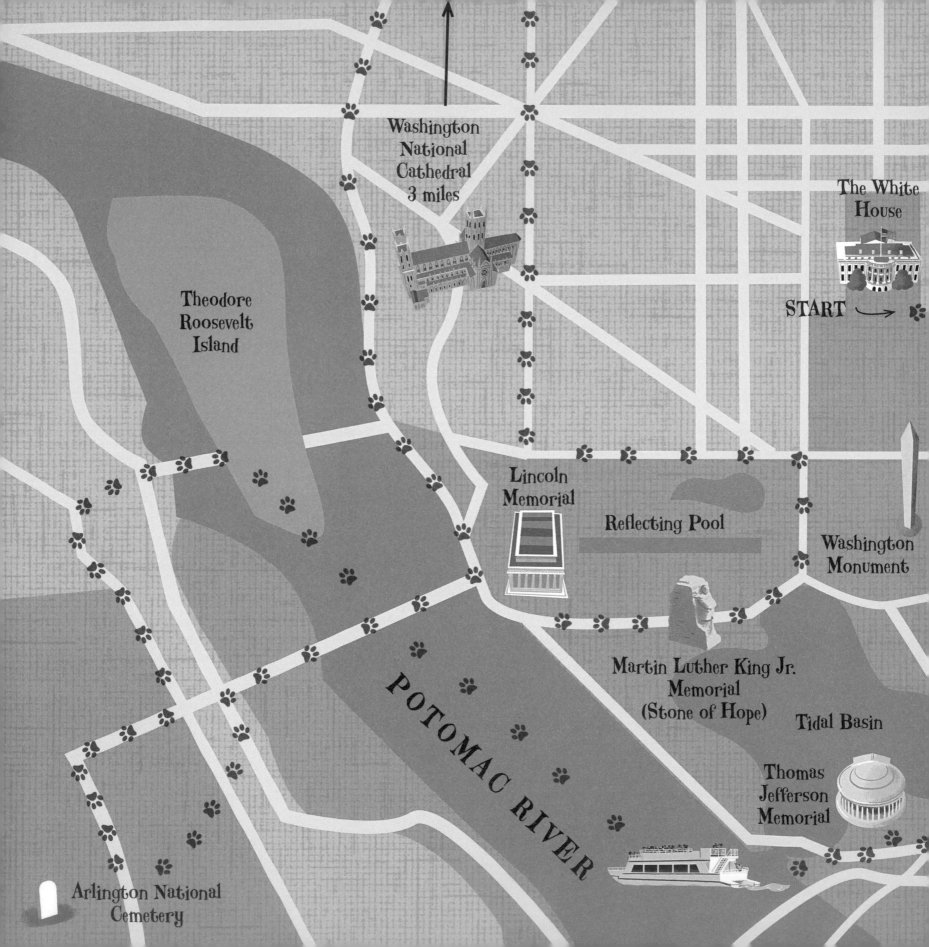